Katie and the Bathers

James Mayhew

ORCHARD BOOKS

For little Katie Light

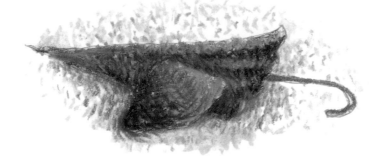

and for Vanessa Hadfield
and Liz Johnson
(I couldn't have done it without you!)

ORCHARD BOOKS
96 Leonard Street, London EC2A 4XD
Orchard Books Australia
32/45-51 Huntley Street, Alexandria, NSW 2015
First published in Great Britain in 2004
First paperback publication in 2005
ISBN 1 84121 736 0 (hardback)
ISBN 1 84362 035 9 (paperback)
Text and illustrations © James Mayhew 2004
The right of James Mayhew to be identified as
the author and illustrator of this work has been asserted
by him in accordance with the Copyright, Designs and Patents Act, 1988.
A CIP catalogue record for this book is available from the British Library.
(hardback) 10 9 8 7 6 5 4 3 2 1
(paperback) 10 9 8 7 6 5 4 3 2 1
Printed in Belgium

It was a sunny day, and Katie and Grandma were feeling hot and bothered.

"Let's go swimming," said Grandma. "I'll get our swimsuits."

It was warm and peaceful in the picture – the sun shone, oars splashed and a boy in a red hat called to the boats racing on the river. Katie saw a little bathing hut and decided to change into her swimsuit . . .

Katie found herself in a park where everyone looked very elegant and grand.

"Oh, you are lucky," sighed the little girl. "It's such a hot day but no one is allowed to bathe in this painting."

"Come and paddle in the gallery!"
said Katie. "It's lovely and cool."

"Oh Prudence, please say yes!"
pleaded the girl to her governess.

"Well, be sure to keep your clothes
dry, Josette," said Prudence.

"What a splendid idea!" said the elegant people. "Let's paddle too!"
The ladies hitched up their skirts and the gentlemen rolled up their
trousers, and then they all had a wonderful time paddling in the gallery.

But water was still pouring out of the painting . . .

"It's getting too deep to paddle," said Josette, standing on the steps.

"How will we get back to our picture?" said the elegant people. "We can't swim in these clothes!"

"Let's fetch a boat!" said Katie. She pointed to another picture by Seurat, called *Port of Honfleur*. Katie and Jacques swam over to the painting and quickly clambered inside.

They found a little rowing boat in the harbour.
It was quite heavy but they managed to drag
it over the frame and into the gallery.
Then off they rowed to the rescue!

The kindly washerwoman gave Prudence some clothes to wear and hung out her wet dress to dry. Then Katie, Josette and the washerwoman's daughter played in the sun as the women chatted.

Suddenly, Katie heard Jacques calling from the boat.

"We must get back to our pictures," said Jacques. "The guard is coming!"

"The guard!" gasped Katie. "He'll be horrified when he sees all this water!"

"Quickly! Jump aboard!" called Jacques. Prudence changed back into her clothes and carefully stepped into the boat. Katie and Josette leapt in after her.

Jacques rowed across the gallery while Katie desperately tried to think of a way to get rid of the water. They passed all sorts of pictures; none of them looked very useful. Then Katie saw a painting by Paul Signac called *Portrait of Felix Feneon*.

"He looks like a magician," said Katie, so she yelled, "Excuse me, can you do any magic? The gallery is a mess and the guard is coming!"

Felix wanted to help, so he leant out of the painting, waved his stick over his hat and shouted, "ABRACADABRA!"

Coloured swirls came out of his picture, but the gallery was still flooded.

"I'll try again," he said. "ALLA-KAZAM!"

"Oh dear," said Felix, as stars and rainbows floated into the gallery. "I'm not very good at magic."

Just then, they all heard footsteps. It was the guard!
"Oh, please try once more!" begged Katie.
"ALLA-KAZOOM! Clear up this room!" said Felix.

There was a flash of light and everything vanished in a swirl of stars and colours.

Katie found she was standing in her dry clothes and everyone and everything was back where it belonged – just in time!

The guard looked carefully around the room.
Everything was exactly as it should be.
"Thank you everyone," whispered Katie.
"I've had a wonderful time!"

As soon as the guard had gone, Katie gently woke Grandma.

"Would you like to go swimming now?" yawned Grandma.

"I don't feel quite so hot any more!" laughed Katie.

"In that case, you won't be wanting an ice cream either," said Grandma.

"Oh, I can always manage an ice cream," said Katie.

"Me too!" smiled Grandma. And off they went.

More about the Pointillists

The painters Seurat, Signac and Pissarro were called Pointillists. The Pointillists liked to keep their colours pure and so didn't mix them together before they applied them to the canvas. They painted their pictures entirely in dots, deliberately placing contrasting or complementary colours next to one another to create different effects. This painting style not only kept colours vivid but seemed to capture both the scene and its atmosphere. At the time, many people didn't like Pointillist paintings – perhaps they found them fuzzy or messy – but painting in the Pointillist style took a long time and required a great deal of patience! Today, Pointillism is loved by many.

Georges Seurat (1859-91)

Georges Seurat was the first artist to develop the Pointillist style of painting. If you look closely at his paintings you can see they are made up of brightly coloured dots, but from a distance the coloured dots seem to mix, creating new shades. In this way, Seurat could keep his colours bright, making the pictures rich and lively. *Bathers at Asnières* is an early example of this and you can see it at the National Gallery in London.

Seurat is particularly famous for his paintings of holiday spots, such as *Sunday Afternoon on the Island of La Grande Jatte*, which you can see at The Art Institute of Chicago, USA, or *Port of Honfleur*, which can be seen at The Barnes Foundation in Merion, USA.

Paul Signac (1863-1935)

Paul Signac was a great admirer of Seurat's paintings. Signac also painted in the Pointillist style, but in his later pictures, he applied the paint in mosaic-like squares, instead of dots. *Portrait of Felix Feneon* shows Signac's friend, an important French art critic, against a backdrop of swirling patterns which seems to capture his lively personality. You can see *Portrait of Felix Feneon* at the Museum of Modern Art in New York, USA.

Camille Pissarro (1830-1903)

Camille Pissarro was born in the West Indies but later came to Paris to study art. Camille loved to explore France, and painted the scenes he saw right on the spot, in the open air. He also admired Seurat's ideas and painted in the Pointillist style for several years. His pictures have large brush strokes, blurring into each other, creating a soft, dreamy look. A good example is *Woman Hanging up the Washing*, which you can see at the Musée d'Orsay in Paris, France.

Acknowledgements:

Bathers at Asnières (1884) by Georges Seurat, National Gallery, London, UK/Bridgeman Art Library; Sunday Afternoon on the Island of La Grande Jatte (1884-86) by Georges Seurat, Art Institute of Chicago, IL, USA/Bridgeman Art Library; Port of Honfleur (c.1886) by Georges Seurat, The Barnes Foundation, Merion, Pennsylvania, USA/Bridgeman Art Library; Woman Hanging up the Washing (1887) by Camille Pissarro, Musée d'Orsay, Paris, France/Bridgeman Art Library/Giraudon; Portrait of Felix Feneon in 1890, Against a Background Rhythmic with Beats and Angles, Tones and Colours (1890) by Paul Signac © ADAGP, Paris and DACS, London 2004, Museum of Modern Art, New York, USA/Bridgeman Art Library.